FATHER BEAR COMES HOME

FATHER BEAR COMES HOME

by ELSE HOLMELUND MINARIK

pictures by MAURICE SENDAK

by the author and artist of LITTLE BEAR

SCHOLASTIC INC.

New York   Toronto   London   Auckland   Sydney
Mexico City   New Delhi   Hong Kong   Buenos Aires

ISBN 0-439-37536-3

12 11 10 9 8 7 6 5 4 3   2 3 4 5 6 7/0

Printed in the U.S.A.   23

First Scholastic printing, February 2002

To
URSULA and SUSAN

CONTENTS

LITTLE BEAR AND OWL

"Little Bear," said Mother Bear,

"can you be my fisherman?"

"Yes, I can," said Little Bear.

"Good," said Mother Bear.

"Will you go down

to the river?

Will you catch a fish for us?"

"Yes, I will," said Little Bear.

So Little Bear went down

to the river.

And there he saw Owl.

Owl was sitting on a log.

"Hello, Little Bear," said Owl.

"Hello, Owl," said Little Bear.

"Father Bear is not home.

He is fishing on the ocean.

"But Mother Bear wants a fish now,
so I have to catch one."

"Good," said Owl.

"Catch one."

Little Bear fished.

"I have one," he said.

"Is it too little?"

"It looks good to me," said Owl.

"Well," said Little Bear,

"Father Bear can catch big fish.

He sails in a big boat, too."

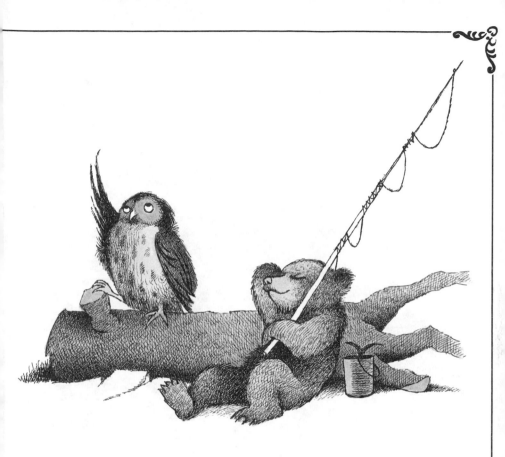

Owl said,

"Someday you will be a big bear.

You will catch big fish.

And you will sail in a boat,

like Father Bear."

13

"I know what," said Little Bear.

"We can make believe.

The log can be a boat.

I will be Father Bear.

"You can be you,
and we are fishing."

"Where are we fishing?" asked Owl.
"On the ocean," said Little Bear.

"All right," said Owl.

"Hurray!" said Little Bear.
"See what I have."

"What is it?" asked Owl.

"An octopus," said Little Bear.

"Oh," said Owl.
"But see what I have."

"What is it?" asked Little Bear.

"A whale," said Owl.

"But a whale is too big,"
said Little Bear.

"This is a little whale," said Owl.

Just then Mother Bear came along.

"Where is the fish?" she asked.

Little Bear laughed. He säid,
"How about an octopus?"
"An octopus!" said Mother Bear.

"Well, then," said Owl,

"how about a little whale?"

"A WHALE!!" said Mother Bear.
"No, thank you. No whale."

"Then how about this fish?"
said Little Bear.

"Yes, thank you," said Mother Bear,
"that is just what I want."

Little Bear said,
"You will see.
When I am as big as Father Bear,
I will catch a real octopus."

"Yes, and sail in a real boat,"
said Owl.

"I know it," said Mother Bear.

Owl said,
"Little Bear fishes very well."

"Oh, yes," said Mother Bear,
"he fishes very well, indeed.

"He is a real fisherman,

just like his father."

21

FATHER BEAR COMES HOME

"Hello, Hen."

"Hello, Little Bear."

"Guess what!" said Little Bear.

"What?"

"Father Bear is coming home today."

"Is he?" said Hen.

"Where was he?"

"Fishing," said Little Bear,

"out on the ocean.

Far out on the ocean."

"My!" said Hen.

"Out on the ocean. Well!"

"Yes," said Little Bear,

"and what if he saw a mermaid?"

"A mermaid!" said Hen.

"Yes, a little mermaid," said Little Bear.
"And maybe she could come home with him."

"Ooh!" said Hen.
"A mermaid at your house.

"I want to see her.

I am coming home with you."

They walked along,

and there was Duck.

"Hello, Duck," said Little Bear.

"Father Bear is coming home today.

Guess where he was."

"Where?" asked Duck.

"Fishing," said Little Bear,
"far out on the ocean.
Out where the mermaids are, maybe."

"Yes," said Hen,
"and we are going to see one."

"What is a mermaid like?"
asked Duck.

"A mermaid!" said Little Bear.
"Why, a mermaid is very pretty.
A mermaid's hair is blue and green.
Like the ocean,
blue and green."

"She is coming home with Father Bear," said Hen.

"Ooh!" said Duck.
"I want to see her, too.
I am coming home with you."

They walked along,

and there was Cat.

"Hello, Cat," said Little Bear.

"Father Bear is coming home today.

He was fishing on the ocean,

far out on the ocean."

"Yes," said Hen,

"out where the mermaids are."

"And," said Duck,

"we are going to see one."

"Where are you going to see one?"
asked Cat.

"One is coming home with Father Bear," said Hen.

"Yes," said Duck,

"and her hair is blue and green."

"And maybe her eyes are silver,"

said Little Bear,

"silver, like the moon."

"Silver eyes!" said Cat.

"How pretty!

I will have to see her.

I am coming home with you."

They walked along,

and there was Little Bear's house.

And there was Father Bear.

He had come home.

Little Bear ran to Father Bear

and hugged him.

Father Bear hugged Little Bear.

Then Father Bear said hello
to Hen, and Duck, and Cat.

"We came to see the mermaid,"
said Hen.

"Her hair is blue and green,"
said Duck.

"Her eyes are silver like the moon,"
said Cat.

"And she is very pretty," said Hen.

"How nice!" said Father Bear.

"Where is she?"

"You have her,"
said Hen and Duck and Cat.

"Oh?" said Father Bear.

35

He looked at Little Bear.

"No mermaid?" asked Little Bear.

"No little mermaid?"

"No," said Father Bear,

"no little mermaid."

"Well!" said Hen.

"My!" said Duck.

"Really!" said Cat.

They all looked at Little Bear.

"But I said maybe," said Little Bear,
"I did say maybe."

"Come, now," said Father Bear.

"See what I have for all of you.

Sea shells.

You can hear the ocean in them.

And maybe you can hear the mermaids, too.

Maybe."

HICCUPS

Little Bear was happy.

Father Bear was home.

He was in his chair reading.

Cat, Duck, Hen and Little Bear
were playing with the sea shells.
They were trying to hear the ocean.

"I hear it," said Cat.

"So do I," said Duck.

"I do, too," said Hen.

"I do, hic—too," said Little Bear.

"Hic!" he said again.

"You have the hiccups," said Cat.

"Have some water, Little Bear,"
said Mother Bear.

So Little Bear had some water,
but he did not stop hiccuping.

"Hello, everyone!"

Owl was at the door.

"Hello, Owl," said Mother Bear,

"you are the very one for us.

You are always so wise.

Water will not stop Little Bear's hiccups.

What can we do?"

"Well, now," said Owl,

"water is very good,

but he must hold his breath, too."

"Hic," said Little Bear.

"Hic, how can I—hic—

hold my—hic—breath, too?

Hic?"

"You can," said Owl.

"Try."

Little Bear did as Owl said.

"See?" said Little Bear.

"No more hic—hic—hiccups."

He was hiccuping again.

"This always works," said Cat.

And he gave Little Bear

a slap on the back.

"Oof!" said Little Bear. "Hic!

That's not—hic—any good."

45

"Someone is by the door,"
said Cat.

"Someone is coming in."

Little Bear laughed.

"Look at—hic—that," he said.

"It's—hic—only Duck and Hen."

"Did we make the hiccups go away?"
asked Duck.

"No—hic—you did not,"
said Little Bear.

Father Bear roared—

"There is too much noise here.

Who is making all that noise?"

He looked at Owl, Cat, Hen and Duck.

"How can I read with all that noise?"

he asked.

And he looked at Little Bear.

"Noise?" said Little Bear.

"I was only hiccuping."

"What was that?" said Father Bear.

"Hiccuping," said Little Bear.
"I was only hiccuping."

Father Bear laughed.
"Hiccuping!" he said.

"I can't hear any hiccups."

"But I was hiccuping," said Little Bear.

"All right," said Father Bear,
"hiccup for me."

But Little Bear could not do it.

"Come, now," said Father Bear.

"One, two, three, hiccup."

No, Little Bear could not do it.

"Well, well," said Father Bear.

"I guess he can't hiccup any more."

52

"Why should he?" said Mother Bear.

"Who wants hiccups anyway?" said Hen.

"That's right," said Cat and Duck.

"Who wants hiccups?"

Owl said,

"You can still stop them my way.

Little Bear didn't really try."

They all laughed,
and Owl laughed, too.

"You just have to know how to do it,"
said Owl.

"That's right," said Father Bear.
"You just have to know how to do it."

LITTLE BEAR'S MERMAID

"We can picnic here," said Mother Bear.

"It is nice here, by the river."

"Let's go for a swim," said Father Bear.

Owl said,

"Little Bear swims like a fish."

"Yes," said Little Bear,

"but mermaids swim best of all.

I still wish we had a mermaid.

Maybe there is a mermaid in the river."

"I never saw one," said Cat.

"Well," said Little Bear,

"she may be shy.

She may not want us to see her.

If we could make believe we are asleep,

she might come and look at us."

"Would she like us?" asked Hen.

"Of course," said Little Bear.

"She might want to play with you," said Mother Bear.

58

"Then I would jump up
and play with her," said Little Bear.

"Oh," said Owl,
"but if she is shy,
she might jump back in the river.
Then all we could see
would be bubbles."

"I see some bubbles now,"

said Little Bear.

"And where there are bubbles,

there may be a mermaid.

I'm going in."

"If you find a mermaid,"

said Father Bear,

"ask her to picnic with us."

"Yes, do that," said Mother Bear.

"Ask her."

61

"I will," said Little Bear,

"because you never can tell.

She might really come back with me."

"Yes indeed," said Father Bear,

"she might really come back with you.

Because you never can tell

about mermaids.

You never can tell."